Catty Jane
Who Loved to Dance

Written and illustrated by
VALERI GORBACHEV

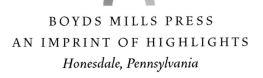

BOYDS MILLS PRESS
AN IMPRINT OF HIGHLIGHTS
Honesdale, Pennsylvania

Boyds Mills Press
An Imprint of Highlights
815 Church Street
Honesdale, Pennsylvania 18431

Printed in China
ISBN: 978-1-59078-982-7
Library of Congress Control Number: 2013932842

First edition
The text of this book is set in Caxton.
The drawings are done in watercolor and pen and ink.

10 9 8 7 6 5 4 3 2 1

To my son, Koseya, and my daughter, Sasha
—*VG*

Catty Jane loved to dance.

Every morning she leaped up and jetéd through her day
until it was time to pirouette back into bed.

As a baby, she danced in her crib.

As a toddler, she danced before she could walk.

As a child, she dreamed of becoming a real ballerina someday.

At long last, Mama decided that Catty Jane was old enough to take ballet lessons at Mrs. Herron's Dance Academy.

"You are doing well for your first class, Catty Jane," said Mrs. Herron. "Remember that becoming a ballerina takes a lot of practice."

"Then I will practice, practice, practice!" said Catty Jane.
And she danced all the way home.

Froggy was waiting for Catty Jane on his front steps.

"Where have you been?" he cried. "I've been sitting here for ages! Come play soccer with me."

"Sorry, but I can't," said Catty Jane. "I'm too busy."

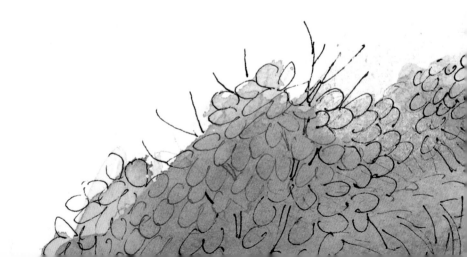

"What are you busy with?" Froggy asked.
"I'm now a student at Mrs. Herron's
Dance Academy," Catty Jane announced,
"so I need to practice, practice, practice. I'm
going to be a real ballerina. Look, Froggy!"
And she showed him her dance.

"I'm going to be a ballet dancer too," said Froggy.
"Catty Jane, do you like my dance?"

"No," said Catty Jane.
Froggy frowned. "I think I'm a very good ballet dancer."

"You vaulted and you somersaulted and your dance doesn't look like ballet at all," said Catty Jane.

"I'm not your friend anymore!" yelled Froggy.
"Fine!" cried Catty Jane. "I'm not your friend either!"
In a huff, Catty Jane and Froggy plopped down on the bench in Froggy's yard.

Just then, along came Piggy and Goose.
"What's wrong?" asked Piggy.
"What happened?" asked Goose.

"Froggy is angry because he is not a great dancer like I am,"
said Catty Jane.

"That's not true," cried Froggy. "I can dance better than Catty Jane!"

"You're both great dancers," said Goose.

"Let's have a dance party," said Piggy.

"I'm too busy," said Catty Jane. "I'm a serious student at Mrs. Herron's Dance Academy. I must practice, practice, practice."

And she left.

Catty Jane couldn't wait to practice ballet.

She didn't even go inside her house.

She practiced on her porch.

She twirled and she whirled. Catty Jane loved pirouetting. But the dance party was loud. She heard peals of laughter and happy voices.

Catty Jane looked over at her friends in Froggy's yard. Goose and Piggy wiggled and wobbled. Froggy vaulted and somersaulted. They were not doing ballet, but their dancing was funny and friendly, just like Goose, Piggy, and Froggy.

"Catty Jane, why are you alone on the porch
while your friends are having fun across the street?"
Mama asked.

Catty Jane didn't answer.

She leaped off the porch. "Froggy!" she called. "You are not a ballet dancer, but you *are* a great dancer."

"Catty Jane," said Froggy, "come dance with us!"

And she did.
Mama brought her delicious cookies and played her saxophone.
Catty Jane practiced ballet . . . with her friends. They all danced in different ways. They all danced together.

They danced for the rest of the day.